EGMONT

We bring stories to life

This edition published in Great Britain 2011 by Dean,
an imprint of Egmont UK Limited
239 Kensington High Street, London W8 6SA
All Rights Reserved

HiT entertainment

ISBN 978 0 6035 6416 1
5 7 9 10 8 6 4
Printed and bound in Malaysia

Thomas and
the Circus

The engines were very excited,
the circus was coming to the
Island of Sodor!

Percy was looking forward to
seeing the clever, dancing horses.

James couldn't wait to see
the funny clowns with their big
shoes and bright red noses.

And Thomas? He just wanted
to see the big-top tent go up!

All the engines wanted to be chosen to go to the Docks to collect the circus, but who would The Fat Controller ask?

It was Thomas! He was excited.

"But, Thomas," The Fat Controller said. "If there are too many trucks for you to pull, you must share the work with the other engines."

"Yes, Sir, I will," said Thomas, and he steamed off happily with Annie and Clarabel.

At the Docks, Cranky the Crane had loaded the circus train. There were horse boxes and costumes and people everywhere.

The acrobats and clowns climbed aboard Annie, and Clarabel carried the Ringmaster and the band.

Salty shunted the very long,
very heavy circus train into place
behind Thomas. "Need any help,
matey?" Salty asked.

Thomas remembered what The Fat
Controller had said about sharing
the work, but he wanted to pull
the circus train all by himself.

"No, thank you, Salty," he said.
"I can do it!"

Then Thomas took the biggest puff
he could and slowly chuff-chuffed
out into the countryside.

Thomas wanted to do a good
job, and he had to work very
hard indeed.

His pistons pumped
and his traction
rods rattled.
But Thomas was
so happy that
he took no notice.
"Peep, peep!"

When Thomas pulled the circus train through Maron Station, he got a lovely surprise. The platforms were full of people waving and cheering!

The circus performers waved back, and the band played a cheerful song.

Thomas was so happy that
he joined in by blowing his whistle:
"Peep, peep!"

When Thomas had to stop at the
junction, children lined the bridge
to wave and cheer.

"Peep!" Thomas blew his whistle
extra loudly for them.

Percy chuffed alongside Thomas.
He really wanted to help.
"Is there anything I can take for you,
Thomas?" he asked.

But Thomas wanted to do
everything himself. He was having
too much fun on his own to accept
help from Percy.

"No, thank you, Percy," he said.
"I'll do it on my own."

"Oh, I see," Percy said, disappointed,
as he watched Thomas chuff away.

Thomas puffed on, and on, and on.

The train felt heavier, and heavier, and heavier.

His traction rods rattled, and rattled, and rattled!

When he stopped at a signal, James was waiting in the siding.

Like Percy, James wanted to help with the circus train.

"If you uncouple some trucks, I can take them for you," James offered.

But Thomas still didn't want any help, even though he was tired.

"No, thank you, James," he said. "I can do it on my own."

Thomas steamed off again, but the load was heavy and his axles ached. Every puff was harder, and every chuff made him feel more and more tired.

When Thomas passed through the next station he didn't even have

enough steam to whistle to the people waving from the platform.

He couldn't manage even one single tiny toot. He was almost all out of puff.

Then, out in the countryside - creak! crack! - Thomas' traction rods broke, and he stopped with a jolt. He couldn't move!

Thomas was very worried, and so were the circus performers.

"We need to practise," said one of
the clowns.

"And the horses need more hay,"
said the Ringmaster.

Thomas' Driver telephoned for help
and soon James arrived with new
traction rods.

Percy brought some hay for the
horses, too.

Thomas was very sorry to have
caused a delay.

"I wanted to keep all the fun
to myself," said Thomas.
"But now I wish I had shared the
work with you."

"Never mind, we'll all have fun
now!" puffed Percy, kindly.

Thomas had his new traction rods fitted. Then he was uncoupled from the trucks.

Percy and James took the dancing horses and the funny clowns.

And Thomas took the band and the big-top tent.

Then the band started playing and
the circus train set off again.

Percy was right! Sharing the work
was much more fun!

Now, when people waved and
cheered, three engines blew
their whistles.

Later on, when the circus had been
set up, the engines went to look
at the big-top tent.

"Thank you, for helping me!" peeped Thomas, to James and Percy. "Sharing work is good because it makes the job easier. But sharing fun with your friends is even better!"